MEAN GIRLS™

Totally Fetch
MOCKTAILS

Parragon.

CONTENTS

THE RULES OF MOCKTAILS

These mocktails aren't regular mocktails...they're cool mocktails. And with twists on classic cocktails and mixology techniques, this book teaches you how to make them.

Glassware

Highball Glass
Sometimes also known as a collins glass, these glasses are perfect for serving tall, cool drinks in style.

Lowball Glass
The lowball glass, also known as a rocks glass, is a short, squat tumbler and is great for a smaller beverage with a classy garnish.

Champagne Flute
The tall, thin flute's tapered design helps keep fizz in a drink longer.

Hurricane Glass
This pear-shaped glass pays homage to the hurricane lamp. It's also an excellent glass for a variety of frozen and blended mocktails.

Iced Beverage Glass
A variation on the highball glass that combines a tapered, tall bowl with a short stem, this glass is ideal for serving chilled drinks.

Mule Mug
Traditionally made of copper, this mug is not only aesthetically pleasing but keeps mixed drinks chilled to perfection.

Pitcher
Although not strictly a glass, a pitcher or jug is a great addition to your mocktail glassware. Mocktails are perfect drinks to be shared with friends and family and a good pitcher is an easy way to ensure there is enough for everyone.

Ingredients

Any mixed drink relies on an appropriate combination of ingredients to endow it with mixology magic, and there is a wide variety of ingredients suitable for making quality mocktails.

Juices
Juices range from freshly squeezed and store-bought brands to pulps and fruit nectars. You can make your own juices at home using an electric juicer, a hand juicer, or even just by giving the fruit sections a good squeeze by hand. Freshly squeezed juice will need to be strained to remove any bits.

Syrups

A syrup is a combination of sugar and water. They're used all over the world by mixologists, baristas, and chefs to sweeten and add flavor to their creations. Some of the mocktail recipes here tell you how to make your own syrups; others use store-bought syrups.

Shrubs

A shrub is a sweet but tart liquid traditionally made with fruit, sugar, and vinegar. Shrubs are easy to make at home, and for mocktail lovers they're also quite versatile. The mocktail recipes here tell you how to make your own shrubs.

Tea and Coffee

There are many uses for tea within mocktails, including infusions, chilled tea, and tea syrups. Coffee has grown in popularity as an ingredient in mixed drinks and there are many ways to use coffee in mocktails from using the beans as a garnish to using iced coffee as an ingredient to create coffee-flavored syrups.

Purees

A puree is an easy way to enhance a mocktail with fruity flavors without needing to muddle fruit directly into your mixed drink. To make your own puree at home, place fruit in a blender with sugar and lemon juice and process for 30 seconds. Strain the liquid through a sieve and discard the solids.

Herbs and Spices

Fresh herbs and spices have found their way into the land of delicious mocktails. There are many ways to use these fragrant ingredients, like mint, in infusions, syrups, and shrubs.

Eggs

Egg whites are used in mocktails to help create foams in various thicknesses, from a light froth to a heavy, creamy foam. For a simple foam, egg white, lemon juice, and sugar are used. The fresher the egg white, the more stable the foam. Egg yolks are used to create a depth of richness to a drink.

Allergies

Food allergies? Don't sweat. You can still enjoy everything this book has to offer. Try these subs in your mocktails:

- Eggs: aquafaba (chickpea water) is a great swap that gives foamy results.
- Fruit: substitute another fruit or fruit juice. Most recipes are pretty versatile!
- Nuts: a nut-free toffee syrup can replace a nut-flavored syrup.

If you have serious allergies, always read the ingredient list of each of the products you use. For more detailed information on ingredients and allergies, please see our Note for the Reader on page 160.

CHAPTER ONE

WELCOME TO NORTH SHORE HIGH SCHOOL

In this section you'll find mocktails that embrace fresh produce and ingredients that are cool and refreshing... much like the promise of the first day of school.

Cady's Big Day

SERVES 12

24 ounces apple juice
12 ounces lemon juice
4 ounces simple syrup
64 ounces ginger ale
orange slices, to garnish

1. Pour the apple juice into a large pitcher.

2. Add the lemon juice, simple syrup, and a handful of ice cubes.

3. Add the ginger ale and stir gently to mix.

4. Pour into chilled lowball glasses and garnish with orange slices.

HOMESCHOOLED

SERVES 1

2¼ ounces hazelnut syrup
sparkling water
lime slice, to garnish

1. Fill a chilled collins glass with ice.

2. Pour the hazelnut syrup over the ice and fill with sparkling water. Stir gently and garnish with a slice of lime.

"So you've actually never been to a real school before?

Shut up! Shut up!"

Hello, High School

SERVES 6

2 ounces fresh mint
3 ounces simple syrup
16 ounces grapefruit
  juice
6 ounces lemon juice
sparkling water
fresh mint sprigs,
  to garnish

"THE FIRST DAY OF SCHOOL WAS A BLUR... A STRESSFUL, SURREAL BLUR."

Muddler: This miniature masher is used for crushing ingredients, such as herbs, in the bottom of a glass. You can also use a mortar and pestle.

1. Muddle fresh mint leaves in a small bowl with the simple syrup.

2. Set aside for at least two hours to steep, mashing again from time to time.

3. Strain the steeped mixture into a pitcher and add the grapefruit juice and lemon juice. Cover with plastic wrap and chill for at least two hours.

4. To serve, fill six chilled collins glasses with ice. Divide the grapefruit mixture evenly in the glasses, then top with sparkling water. Garnish with fresh mint.

Strainer: A bar strainer prevents ice and other ingredients from being poured from the shaker or mixing glass into the serving glass. You could use a small nylon strainer instead.

Ms. Norbury

*Like this mixed-bag drink, Ms. Norbury is
a little bit messy but good at heart.*

SERVES 6

16 ounces lemonade, chilled
15 ounces cola, chilled
15 ounces dry ginger ale,
   chilled
juice of 1 orange
juice of 1 lemon
few drops nonalcoholic
   aromatic bitters
sliced fruit, such as apples,
   strawberries, and oranges
fresh mint sprigs

1. Mix the first six ingredients
   together thoroughly in a large
   pitcher or punch bowl.

2. Float in the fruit and mint.
   Keep the mixture in the
   refrigerator and add the ice
   cubes just before serving.

PRINCIPAL DUVALL

This classic drink is as straightforward as Principal Duvall.

SERVES 1

4½ ounces lemonade
4½ ounces iced tea

1. Fill a chilled highball glass halfway with ice cubes and pour in the lemonade.

2. Slowly pour in the tea, so it does not mix.

3. Serve with a straw.

"I WILL KEEP YOU HERE ALL NIGHT."

"WE CAN'T KEEP THEM PAST FOUR."

"I WILL KEEP YOU HERE TILL FOUR."

CARPAL TUNNEL

SERVES 1

6 ounces apple juice
1 teaspoon simple syrup
½ teaspoon lemon juice
sparkling water
apple slice, to garnish

1. Shake the apple juice, simple syrup, and lemon juice vigorously in a cocktail shaker filled with ice until well frosted.

2. Strain into a chilled tumbler and top with sparkling water. Garnish with a slice of apple.

Cocktail shaker: These come in several sizes and are used to mix the ingredients of a drink by shaking. Some come with a perforated strainer—if yours does not have an integral strainer, you will need a separate one.

New Student

SERVES 4

1 pineapple
3½ cups water
1 ounce fresh mint
2-inch piece of fresh ginger, peeled and finely sliced
4 ounces agave syrup
2 tablespoons fresh mint leaves, to garnish

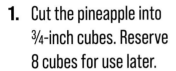

This recipe requires additional time for cooling and infusing—plan accordingly.

1. Cut the pineapple into ¾-inch cubes. Reserve 8 cubes for use later.

2. Pour the water into a large saucepan and add the pineapple, mint, and ginger. Stir in the agave syrup and place the saucepan over a medium-high heat. Simmer for 45 minutes, or until the liquid has reduced by half.

3. Remove from the heat and allow the nectar to cool completely and flavors to infuse. This will take 4–5 hours. Using a slotted spoon, remove the mint sprigs and ginger.

4. Add ice, mint leaves, and reserved pineapple cubes to the bottom of a large pitcher. Pour the cooled nectar over the ice and stir to mix.

TWELFTH GRADE
CALCULUS

SERVES 1

6 ounces apple juice
1 small scoop vanilla
  ice cream
sparkling water
cinnamon sugar, to garnish
apple slice, to garnish

1. Put 4–6 ice cubes into a blender, then add the apple juice and ice cream.

2. Blend for 10–15 seconds until frothy and frosted. Pour into a glass and top with sparkling water.

3. Sprinkle the cinnamon sugar on top and garnish with an apple slice.

"I like math."

"Ew, why?"

"Because it's
the same in
every country."

"That's beautiful.
This girl
is deep."

"She's the queen bee, the star.

Those other two are just her little workers."

Queen Bee

SERVES 2

2 ripe nectarines, pitted
  and quartered
7 ounces 2% milk
2 tablespoons Greek yogurt
1 tablespoon bee pollen
1 teaspoon honey
1 teaspoon bee pollen,
  to garnish
2 slices nectarine,
  to garnish

1. Place the nectarines, milk, yogurt, bee pollen, and honey in a blender and blend until smooth. Add the ice cubes and blend again until completely combined.

2. Pour the milkshake into chilled glasses and garnish with the bee pollen and a fresh slice of nectarine.

GO LIONS

SERVES 1

3 ounces carrot juice
4¼ ounces half-and-half or
   heavy cream
3 ounces orange juice
1 egg yolk
orange slice, to garnish

1. Pour the carrot juice,
   cream, and orange juice
   over ice in a shaker, then
   add the egg yolk. Shake
   vigorously until well mixed.

2. Strain into a chilled
   glass and garnish with
   the slice of orange.

The *Plastics*

SERVES 1

3 ounces apple juice
3 ounces grapefruit juice
1 dash grenadine
lime slice, to garnish

1. Shake the apple juice, grapefruit juice, and dash of grenadine in a cocktail shaker over ice cubes until well frosted.

2. Strain into a chilled cocktail glass. Garnish with a lime slice.

Girl World

SERVES 1

6 ounces apple juice
juice of 1 lemon
juice of 1 lime
1½ ounces honey
1 egg white
4–5 raspberries
long apple peel strip,
   to garnish

1. Blend the apple juice, lemon and lime juices, honey, and egg white with ice in a blender until frothy and slushy.

2. Put the raspberries in the bottom of a chilled glass, crush with a wooden spoon, and pour in the fruit slush.

3. Garnish with a strip of apple peel.

"GIRL WORLD HAS A LOT OF RULES."

CHAPTER TWO

On Wednesdays We Wear Pink

On Wednesdays we drink pink, too. In addition to looking pretty, these mocktails also share a variety of zingy flavors perfect for any day of the week...not just Wednesdays.

Regina

This drink presents as sweet and feminine, but is actually a little high maintenance with a sour kick—much like Regina George.

SERVES 8–10

8 fresh mint sprigs,
   to garnish (optional)
sparkling or still water,
   to serve

Pomegranate and Rose Syrup

juice of 2 lemons
¼ teaspoon rose water
7 ounces fresh
   pomegranate juice (juice
   of about 2 pomegranates)
¾ cup sugar

This recipe includes a syrup—plan to make at home or purchase ready-made from the store.

1. To make the syrup, put the lemon juice, rosewater, pomegranate juice, and sugar in a saucepan, stir and cook over a low heat until the sugar has dissolved.

2. Increase the heat to medium-high, bring to a boil, then reduce the heat to low and simmer for 3–4 minutes. Boiling sugar is very hot, so handle with care and make sure it doesn't bubble over. Leave to cool completely. The syrup will keep in the refrigerator in a sealed container for 3–4 days.

3. Put some crushed ice in a tall glass. Pour a dash of the syrup over the ice and add a sprig of mint, if using. Pour in still or sparkling water to taste, and mix well.

A LITTLE BIT Dramatic

Gretchen

Gretchen Wieners may be the black sheep of The Plastics, but this blackberry mocktail is adored by all.

This recipe includes a syrup that needs to be made ahead of time—plan accordingly.

SERVES 1

9 fresh blackberries
3 teaspoons blood orange juice
4 ounces sparkling water
blood orange slice, to garnish

Lemonade Syrup
4 lemons
½ cup sugar
5 ounces water

1. To make the lemonade syrup, zest and juice the lemons. Add to a saucepan with the sugar and water. Place over medium heat until the sugar has dissolved.

2. Strain the mixture and leave to cool. Then pour into a clean bottle and store in the refrigerator for up to 4 weeks.

3. Muddle 8 of the blackberries in a cocktail shaker with the orange juice.

4. Strain into a highball glass and top with the lemonade syrup and sparkling water.

5. Garnish with the remaining blackberry and a blood orange slice.

"I'm sorry that people are jealous of me, jealous of me,

but I can't help it that I'm popular."

Karen

This foamy mocktail pairs perfectly with someone who's sweet, naive, and has a head full of...air.

SERVES 1

juice of ½ lemon
1 egg white
1 dash grenadine
lemonade
lemon slice, to garnish

1. Shake the lemon juice, egg white, and grenadine together in a cocktail shaker, then strain over the ice cubes in a tall glass.

2. Top with lemonade and garnish with a lemon slice on the rim of the glass.

The Rules of Feminism

SERVES 1

5 teaspoons
pomegranate juice, chilled
4 ounces ginger ale, chilled
1 teaspoon pomegranate seeds,
to garnish

1. Pour the pomegranate juice
into a champagne flute.

2. Top with ginger ale.

3. Garnish with the
pomegranate seeds.

"Irregardless, ex-boyfriends are just off-limits to friends."

How to Spell *Orange*

SERVES 1

1½ ounces lemon juice
1½ ounces orange juice
2–3 strawberries, mashed
1½ ounces strawberry
  syrup
½ egg yolk
1 dash grenadine
strawberry slice, to garnish

1. Place the lemon juice, orange juice, strawberries, strawberry syrup, egg yolk, and grenadine in a cocktail shaker and add ice cubes. Shake vigorously.

2. Strain the mixture into a cocktail glass and garnish with the strawberry slice.

Big Hair

SERVES 1

2¼ ounces raspberry syrup
sparkling apple juice, chilled

1. Put 4–6 ice cubes into a
   mixing glass. Then pour
   in the raspberry syrup.

2. Stir well to chill the
   syrup and strain into
   a chilled wine glass.

3. Top up with sparkling
   apple juice and stir.

*Mixing glass: This is used for making
stirred cocktails. You can use any
large container or pitcher, or you can
buy a professional mixing glass.*

"That's why her hair is SO big, it's full of secrets."

Cool Mom VIRGIN COOLER

SERVES 1

2 teaspoons sugar
lime wedge
2 ounces grenadine
2 ounces fresh lemon or lime juice
lemonade
fresh lemon or lime slices,
    to garnish

1. Pour the sugar on a saucer.
   Rub the rim of a chilled
   highball glass with the lime
   wedge, then twist the glass
   rim into the sugar to frost.
   Fill halfway with ice.

2. Pour the grenadine and citrus
   juice into the ice-filled glass.

3. Top with lemonade and finish
   with slices of lemon or lime.

NO RULES

SERVES 1

juice of 1 lemon or
  ½ pink grapefruit
1 ounce grenadine
zest of ½ lemon
2–3 teaspoons raspberry syrup
sparkling water
maraschino cherry, to garnish

1. Pour the lemon or
   grapefruit juice and
   grenadine into a chilled
   tall collins glass with ice.

2. Add the lemon zest,
   syrup, and sparkling
   water to taste. Garnish
   with a cherry.

"I'M NOT A
REGULAR MOM.
I'M A
COOL
MOM!"

So Fetch

SERVES 1

3 fresh strawberries
2 ounces pineapple juice
2 teaspoons fresh lime juice
3½ ounces nonalcoholic
   ginger beer or ginger ale
½ strawberry, to garnish
lime wedge, to garnish

1. Muddle the strawberries in a mule mug or a highball glass.

2. Add the pineapple juice and lime, and stir well to mix.

3. Add ice cubes, top with the ginger beer, and stir again.

4. Garnish with a strawberry half and a lime wedge.

"Stop trying to make 'fetch' happen. It's not going to happen."

FIFTH SENSE

SERVES 1

4 strawberries
6 raspberries
2 teaspoons fresh lime juice
2 fresh basil leaves
1 teaspoon agave syrup
sparkling water
berry skewer, to garnish

1. Muddle the strawberries, raspberries, lime juice, basil, and agave syrup in a cocktail shaker.

2. Fill the shaker with ice cubes and shake hard.

3. Fill a large wine glass with ice cubes and strain the liquid into the glass.

4. Top with sparkling water and stir gently. Garnish with a berry skewer.

"There's a 30% chance

It's already raining."

Watermelon WEDNESDAY

SERVES 1

2 ounces watermelon puree
½ teaspoon agave syrup
2 teaspoons apple juice
2 ounces ginger ale
thin watermelon slice,
  to garnish

1. Fill a cocktail shaker with ice cubes, add the watermelon puree, agave syrup, and apple juice, and shake vigorously.

2. Strain into a chilled champagne flute and top with ginger ale.

3. Garnish with a watermelon slice.

ARMY PANTS AND FLIP-FLOPS

SERVES 1

3 ounces hazelnut syrup
3 ounces lemon juice
1 teaspoon grenadine
sparkling water
slice of papaya, to garnish

1. Shake the syrup, lemon juice, and grenadine vigorously over ice until well frosted.

2. Fill a tumbler halfway with ice and strain the mixture into the glass.

3. Top with sparkling water. Stir gently and garnish with a slice of papaya.

"I saw Cady Heron wearing army pants and flip-flops,

so I bought army pants and flip-flops."

Teen Royalty

SERVES 2

10 ounces cranberry juice
4 ounces orange juice
2 ounces fresh raspberries
1 tablespoon lemon juice

1. Pour the cranberry juice and orange juice into a blender and blend gently until combined.

2. Add the raspberries and lemon juice and blend until smooth.

3. Strain into glasses and serve.

All-Girls Pool Party

SERVES 1

1½ ounces grenadine
3 ounces orange juice
1½ ounces lemon juice
sparkling water
orange wedge, to garnish

1. Pour the grenadine into an ice-filled glass. Carefully pour the orange juice and lemon juice over the back of a spoon so the layers stay separated.

2. Top with sparkling water and garnish with an orange wedge.

Frosty Strudel

SERVES 4

2 lemons
¾ cup confectioners' sugar
6 ounces frozen
   strawberries
2 drops vanilla extract
2 drops almond extract
sparkling water
sliced strawberries,
   to garnish

1. Cut the ends off the lemons, then scoop out and chop the flesh and remove the seeds.

2. Put the lemon flesh in a blender with the sugar, frozen strawberries, vanilla and almond extracts, and 4–6 ice cubes. Blend for 2–3 minutes.

3. Divide the blended mixture among four glasses. Top with sparkling water and garnish with the sliced strawberry.

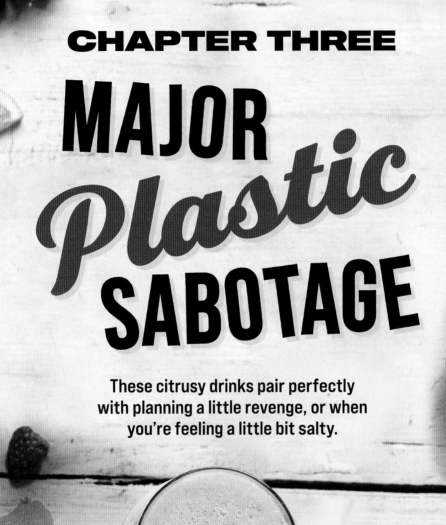

CHAPTER THREE

MAJOR *Plastic* SABOTAGE

These citrusy drinks pair perfectly with planning a little revenge, or when you're feeling a little bit salty.

"At least me and Regina George

know
we're mean!"

JANIS

SERVES 1

2 ounces lime juice

2 teaspoons nonalcoholic aromatic bitters, or to taste

3½ ounces nonalcoholic ginger beer

3½ ounces lemonade

lime slice, to garnish

Like Janis, this drink is a perfect combination of sweet and sour...with just a tad of bitterness.

1. Mix all the ingredients together in a highball glass.

2. Taste and add more bitters if you wish.

3. Add the lime slice to the glass.

Damian

This drink is bright and fun with a sparkling twist, just like Damian.

SERVES 1

2 fresh lemons
peel of ½ lemon
1 tablespoon sugar
sparkling lemonade, chilled

1. Squeeze the fresh lemons and pour the juice into a chilled highball glass filled with crushed ice.

2. Add the lemon peel and sugar to taste and stir briefly.

3. Top with lemonade to taste.

"I want my pink shirt back!"

EVIL DICTATOR

SERVES 1

3 ounces orange juice
3 ounces bitter lemon
orange and lemon slices,
   to garnish

1. Add ice cubes to a
   chilled tumbler. Pour
   in the orange juice
   and bitter lemon.

2. Stir gently and
   garnish with orange
   and lemon slices.

"How do you overthrow a dictator?

a dictator?

You cut off her resources."

SOCIAL SUICIDE

SERVES 1

1½ ounces apricot juice
1½ ounces lemon juice
3 ounces sparkling
    apple juice
lemon peel twist, to garnish

1. Add ice to a mixing glass. Pour the apricot juice, lemon juice, and apple juice over the ice and stir well.

2. Strain into a chilled highball glass and garnish with a lemon twist.

"Don't let the haters stop you from

doing your
thang."

FACE PUNCH

SERVES 1

1 teaspoon granulated sugar
1 teaspoon kosher salt
lime wedges
¾ ounce lime juice
grapefruit juice

1. Mix the sugar and salt together on a saucer.

2. Rub the rim of a chilled highball glass with the lime wedge and twist the glass rim into the sugar and salt mixture to frost.

3. Fill the glass with ice and add the lime juice. Top with grapefruit juice. Garnish with another lime wedge.

"One time, she punched me in the face. IT WAS AWESOME."

8th Grade *Revenge*

SERVES 1

juice of ½ lime
1 teaspoon salt
¼ lemongrass stalk,
  chopped
2 tablespoons mango juice
7 ounces nonalcoholic
  ginger beer, chilled

1. Dip the rim of a chilled highball glass into the lime juice, then twist the glass rim into the salt to frost.

2. Muddle the lemongrass with the mango juice in a shaker and strain into the glass.

3. Top with the ginger beer.

"YOU CAN'T SIT WITH US."

PLASTIC SABOTAGE

SERVES 1

3 ounces chilled fresh
  orange juice
confectioners' sugar
juice of half a lime
few drops nonalcoholic
  aromatic bitters
3–4½ ounces sparkling water

1. Dip the rim of a flute into the orange or lime juice, then dip into the confectioners' sugar.

2. Stir the rest of the juices together with the bitters and then pour into the glass.

3. Add sparkling water to taste.

AXE WOUND

SERVES 1

¾ ounce nonalcoholic bitters
3¾ ounces blood orange juice
sparkling water
orange slice, to garnish
fresh mint sprig, to garnish

1. Pour the bitters into a chilled highball glass filled with ice.

2. Add the blood orange juice. Do not stir.

3. Top with sparkling water.

4. Garnish with the orange slice and mint.

Army of Skanks

SERVES 10

40 ounces grape juice, chilled
10 ounces orange juice, chilled
2½ ounces cranberry juice, chilled
2 ounces lemon juice
2 ounces lime juice
3½ ounces simple syrup
lemon, orange, and lime slices, to garnish

1. Put the grape juice, orange juice, cranberry juice, lemon juice, lime juice, and simple syrup into a chilled punch bowl and stir well.

2. Add ice and garnish with the slices of lemon, orange, and lime.

"Hot" Body

SERVES 1

juice of ½ orange
juice of 1 lime
5 ounces pineapple juice
4–5 drops nonalcoholic aromatic
 bitters
sparkling water or ginger ale,
 to taste
fruit slices, to garnish

1. Shake the first four ingredients
 well together with ice.

2. Strain into a chilled glass
 and fill with sparkling water
 or ginger ale to taste.

3. Finish with a few more drops
 of bitters to taste, garnish
 with slices of fruit.

"It burned down in 1987."

THE BACK BUILDING

SERVES 4

8½ cups white grape juice
¼ ounce (about 40) food-grade
  juniper berries
2 teaspoons agave syrup
8 teaspoons fresh lime juice
20 fresh mint leaves
4 fresh mint sprigs, to garnish
8 juniper berries, to garnish

*This recipe requires additional time
for infusing—plan accordingly.*

1. Pour the grape juice into
   a pitcher. Add the juniper
   berries, stir well, then leave
   to infuse for 3 hours. Strain
   the juice into a clean bottle
   and store in the refrigerator
   for up to one month.

2. Mix the agave syrup
   and lime juice in a julep
   cup or highball glass to
   dissolve the syrup.

3. Bruise the mint leaves
   and add to the cup.

4. Fill the cup with crushed
   ice, then pour in 4 ounces of
   the infused grape juice. Stir
   the mixture through the ice.

5. Top with more crushed ice,
   garnish each glass with a mint
   sprig and two juniper berries.

Sorry, Regina

SERVES 1

½ large avocado
pinch of salt
2½ tablespoons fresh
   lime juice
2 teaspoons agave syrup
3 fresh thyme sprigs
2 ounces sparkling water

1. Mash the avocado with the salt in a cocktail shaker until smooth.

2. Add ice cubes, lime juice, agave syrup, and 2 thyme sprigs and shake hard.

3. Double strain into a hurricane glass and top with the sparkling water.

4. Garnish with the remaining thyme sprig.

"I am so **SORRY,** Regina. Really, I don't know why I did this."

CHAPTER FOUR

It's October Third

These mocktails are fizzy and smooth, and nice to drink any time but especially when you need a pick-me-up after saying something not so smooth to your crush. Grool.

"All he cares about

is school, his mom, and his friends."

Aaron Samuels

Here's a mocktail that features sweet and wholesome ingredients, topped with something sparkly that mimics the butterflies-in-your-stomach feeling of a new crush.

SERVES 1

4 teaspoons elderflower cordial

2 tablespoons fresh lemon juice

4 ounces unfiltered apple juice

6 fresh mint leaves

3½ tablespoons sparkling water

fresh mint sprig, to garnish

apple fan, to garnish

1. Fill a highball glass with ice cubes and add the cordial, lemon juice, and apple juice. Stir well to mix.

2. Bruise the mint, add to the glass and stir again.

3. Top with sparkling water, garnish with the mint sprig and an apple fan.

High-Status *Man Candy*

SERVES 1

9 ounces boiling water
¼ ounce dried lavender
2¾ ounces sugar
2 ounces fresh lemon juice
5 ounces chilled
  sparkling water
lavender sprig, to garnish

This recipe requires additional time for cooling and infusing—plan accordingly.

1. Put the boiling water into a small pan or heatproof bowl and add the lavender. Then add the sugar and stir to dissolve.

2. Cover and leave in the refrigerator overnight to infuse.

3. Strain into a clean bottle and store in the refrigerator.

4. Fill a highball glass with ice cubes and add 2 ounces of the lavender syrup. Add the lemon juice and stir to mix.

5. Top with sparkling water and garnish with a lavender sprig.

Regina's
EX-BOYFRIEND

This recipe includes a syrup that needs to be made ahead of time and requires additional time for cooling and infusing—plan accordingly.

SERVES 1

2 teaspoons fresh lemon juice
3 fresh mint leaves
4 ounces cold breakfast tea or
   peppermint tea
fresh mint sprig, to garnish
lemon slice, to garnish

Vanilla Syrup
1 split vanilla bean
bottle agave syrup

1. Add the split vanilla bean to the bottle of agave syrup and leave it in the bottle to infuse overnight. The pod can stay in the bottle as you use the infused agave.

2. Put the lemon juice and 2 teaspoons of the syrup into the base of a rocks glass and stir to dissolve the agave.

3. Crush the mint leaves and add to the glass.

4. Fill the glass with ice cubes and pour the tea over the ice.

5. Stir well to mix and garnish with a mint sprig and lemon slice.

So Cute

SERVES 1

6 fresh mint leaves, plus
   extra to garnish
1 teaspoon sugar
3 ounces lemon juice
sparkling water
lemon slice, to garnish

1. Put the mint leaves into a chilled collins or highball glass.

2. Add the sugar and lemon juice.

3. Muddle the mint leaves and stir until the sugar has dissolved.

4. Fill the glass with ice cubes and top with sparkling water. Stir gently and garnish with the fresh mint and lemon slice.

The 10/3

SERVES 1

2 teaspoons apple pie syrup
1 tablespoon fresh lime juice
3½ ounces apple juice
2 ounces nonalcoholic
    ginger beer
lime wedge, to garnish

1. Fill a highball glass with ice cubes and add the syrup.

2. Add the lime and apple juice, stir well, and top with the ginger beer.

3. Garnish with the lime wedge.

"On October 3rd, he asked me what day it was."

Grool

SERVES 1

10 blackberries
1 tablespoon confectioners'
   sugar
juice of ½ lemon
juice of ½ lime
lemonade

1. Reserve a few berries.
   Place the remaining fruit
   in a chilled tumbler with
   the sugar and crush
   until well mashed.

2. Add the fruit juices and a
   few ice cubes, then top with
   lemonade. Garnish with the
   reserved whole berries.

"I meant to say cool,

but then I started to say great."

AFTER-SCHOOL *Tutor*

SERVES 1

3 ounces peach juice
6 ounces cold milk
few drops almond extract
1–2 tablespoons clover honey
1 small egg
toasted almonds, to garnish

1. Shake the first five ingredients together until well frosted.

2. Pour into a large cocktail or wine glass and sprinkle the almonds on top.

Extra Credit

SERVES 2

10 ounces milk
12–14 strawberries, hulled
½ ripe avocado
1½ ounces lemon juice

1. Place all the ingredients except 2 strawberries in a blender and blend for 15–20 seconds, until smooth.

2. Pour into iced tall glasses and garnish each glass with slices of strawberry.

Really Pretty

SERVES 2

4 ounces plain yogurt
8 ounces milk
1 tablespoon rose water
3 tablespoons honey
1 ripe mango, peeled and
    diced
rose petals, to garnish

1. Pour the yogurt and milk into a blender and process until combined. Add the rose water and honey and process until blended, then add the mango and ice cubes and blend until smooth.

2. Pour into chilled glasses. Garnish with rose petals.

"So you agree? You think you're really pretty?"

Berry Sexy

SERVES 1

3¼ ounces raspberries
1½ ounces coconut cream
5 ounces pineapple juice

1. Press the raspberries through a strainer with the back of a spoon and transfer the puree to a blender.

2. Add the crushed ice, coconut cream, and pineapple juice, and blend until smooth, then pour the mixture, without straining, into a chilled lowball glass.

SAT PREP

SERVES 2

2 ounces raspberries
6 ounces cranberry juice
6 ounces raspberry juice
1 small meringue, crumbled
blackberry-flavored
   sparkling water

1. Set aside a couple of raspberries for later. In a blender, blend the rest of the fruit with the juices and crushed ice.

2. Divide the fruit slush between two tall glasses and top with the sparkling water.

3. Garnish with raspberries and the crumbled meringue.

"Every Thursday he thinks she's doing SAT prep, but really she's hooking up with Shane Oman in the projection room above the auditorium. I never told anybody that because I'm such a good friend."

Regulation Hottie

SERVES 1

3 ounces peach juice
1½ ounces lemon juice
sparkling apple juice

1. Pour the peach juice
   and lemon juice into
   a chilled champagne
   flute and stir well.

2. Top with sparkling apple
   juice and stir again.

"You're a regulation hottie.

Own it!"

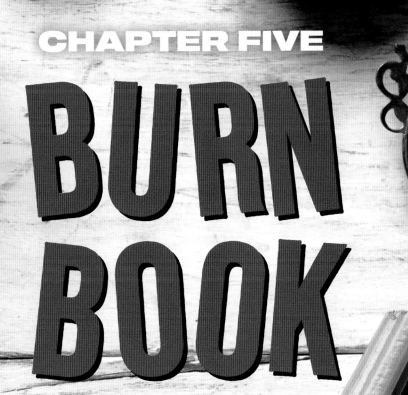

CHAPTER FIVE

BURN BOOK

Not for the faint of heart, these drinks will test your tolerance for spice and heat, much like a little pink book known for delivering similar burns.

"You let it out, honey. **Put it in the** Book."

The Burn Book

SERVES 1

6–8 Padrón or shishito peppers
17 ounces carrot juice
2 teaspoons fresh lemon juice
4 tablespoons fresh orange juice
charred pepper, to garnish
orange twist, to garnish

This recipe requires additional time for cooling and infusing—plan accordingly.

1. Use a chef's blowtorch to char the skins of the peppers.

2. Put the carrot juice in a pitcher. Leaving the charred skins on, add the peppers to the carrot juice, stir the contents, and leave to infuse for 1 hour.

3. Strain and pour the juice into a clean bottle and store in the refrigerator.

4. Fill a rocks glass with ice cubes. Add 3½ ounces of the infused carrot juice, lemon juice, and orange juice, and stir.

5. Garnish with a charred pepper and an orange twist.

Wear gloves when handling hot peppers, and do not touch your face without washing your hands.

NICE WIG

SERVES 1

7 ounces tonic water
2 tablespoons hot or chilled
  espresso

Juniper Syrup
10–15 food-grade
  juniper berries
8½ ounces water
3 tablespoons sugar

*This recipe includes a
syrup that needs to be
made ahead of time—
plan accordingly.*

1. To make the juniper syrup,
   add the juniper berries to a
   saucepan with the water and
   sugar and bring to the boil.

2. Remove from the heat and
   leave to cool, then strain
   into a clean bottle and
   store in the refrigerator.

3. Fill a highball glass with ice
   cubes. Add 2 teaspoons of
   the juniper syrup, pour in the
   tonic water, and gently stir.

4. Place a spoon against the inside
   edge of the glass and slowly
   pour the espresso over the
   back of the spoon to float.

"NICE WIG, JANIS. WHAT'S IT MADE OF?"

"YOUR MOM'S CHEST HAIR."

"I spent about 80% of my time talking about Regina. And the other 20% of the time, I was praying for someone else to bring her up so I could talk about her more."

Obsession

SERVES 1

¼ teaspoon ground turmeric
7 ounces tonic water
2 teaspoons fresh lemon juice
lemon slice, to garnish

1. Add ice cubes and turmeric to a highball glass.

2. Pour in the tonic water and lemon juice and stir well.

3. Garnish with the lemon slice.

HALLOWEEN PARTY

SERVES 1

3 ounces passion fruit syrup
1½ ounces lime juice
bitter lemon
lemon slice, to garnish

1. Pour the passion fruit syrup and lime juice over ice in a mixing glass.

2. Stir well to mix and strain into a chilled tumbler.

3. Top with bitter lemon and dress with a slice of lemon.

Three-Way CALLING ATTACK

SERVES 1

2¾ ounces cold lapsang
   souchong (smoked) tea
3½ ounces tomato juice
2 teaspoons fresh
   lemon juice
3 dashes Worcestershire
   sauce
2 dashes hot sauce
pinch of black pepper
pinch of Himalayan pink salt
lemon slice, to garnish
halved cherry tomato,
   to garnish

1. Add all ingredients except garnishes into a tall glass filled with ice cubes.

2. Stir well. Garnish with a lemon slice and a cherry tomato.

HIT BY A BUS

SERVES 1

1 ounce raw beet, peeled
6 ounces tomato juice
1 teaspoon Worcestershire
 sauce
¼ teaspoon celery salt
¼ teaspoon black pepper
1 teaspoon horseradish,
 freshly grated
½ teaspoon hot sauce
1 lemon slice, to garnish
celery stick, to garnish

*Barspoon: This long-handle
spoon is used for stirring
drinks in a mixing glass.*

1. Cut the beet into small pieces. Place in a cocktail shaker and crush thoroughly with a muddler or pestle to release the color and flavor.

2. Add the tomato juice, Worcestershire sauce, celery salt, pepper, horseradish, and hot pepper sauce. Stir well with a barspoon.

3. Pour the mixture into a collins or highball glass. Add some ice cubes and stir again.

4. Garnish the drink with the lemon slice and celery stick.

Frenemy

SERVES 6

16 ounces tomato juice
8 ounces orange juice
4½ ounces lime juice
¾ ounce hot sauce
2 teaspoons Worcestershire
   sauce
1 jalapeño, seeded and
   finely chopped
celery salt and white pepper

1. Pour the tomato juice, orange juice, lime juice, hot sauce, and Worcestershire sauce into a pitcher.

2. Add the chopped jalapeño and season to taste with the celery salt and white pepper.

3. Stir well, cover, and chill in the refrigerator for at least an hour.

4. To serve, fill 6 highball glasses halfway with ice and strain the cocktail evenly into the glasses.

Wear gloves when handling hot peppers, and do not touch your face without washing your hands.

STAB CAESAR

SERVES 1

1½ ounces lime juice
1½ ounces barbecue sauce
1 dash Worcestershire sauce
1 dash hot sauce
tomato juice
lime slices, to garnish

1. Shake the lime juice, barbecue sauce, Worcestershire sauce, and hot sauce over ice cubes until well frosted.

2. Pour into a chilled highball glass, top with tomato juice, and stir.

3. Garnish with a couple slices of lime.

"GRETCHEN WIENERS HAD CRACKED."

LITTLE SKEEZ

SERVES 2

16 ounces carrot juice
1 ounce watercress
1 tablespoon lemon juice
fresh watercress sprigs,
   to garnish

1. Pour the carrot juice into a blender. Add the watercress and lemon juice and process until smooth.

2. Transfer to a pitcher, cover with plastic wrap, and chill in the refrigerator for at least 1 hour.

3. Pour into glasses and garnish with watercress.

PUSHER

SERVES 2

8 ounces carrot juice
4 tomatoes, peeled, seeded,
   and roughly chopped
1 tablespoon lemon juice
1 ounce fresh parsley
1 tablespoon grated
   fresh ginger
4 ounces water
chopped parsley, to garnish

1. Put the carrot juice, tomatoes, and lemon juice into a blender and process gently until combined.

2. Add the parsley, ginger, and ice cubes. Process until well combined, pour in the water, and process until smooth.

3. Pour the mixture into tall glasses and garnish with the chopped parsley.

"I'm a pusher, Cady. I'm a pusher."

"HOW MANY OF YOU HAVE EVER FELT **PERSONALLY VICTIMIZED** BY REGINA GEORGE?"

Personally Victimized

SERVES 1

2 ounces espresso
1 teaspoon vanilla extract
6 ounces Dr. Pepper

1. In a mixing glass, stir the espresso and vanilla together with ice.

2. Fill a glass with ice and pour in the Dr. Pepper. Pour the espresso mix over the top and stir gently.

Is Butter a Carb?

SERVES 8

½ cup butter, softened
2 cups brown sugar
1 teaspoon ground
    cinnamon
½ teaspoon ground nutmeg
⅛ teaspoon ground
    cardamom
pinch of ground cloves
4 cups boiling water or hot
    apple cider (½ cup of
    either for each drink)
splash of half-and-half or
    heavy cream, optional
ground cinnamon, to garnish

1. To make the buttered spice mixture, combine the butter, sugar, cinnamon, nutmeg, cardamom, and cloves in a mixing bowl. Mix until fully combined.

2. To make each drink, scoop 1½–2 tablespoons of the buttered spice mixture into a small mug. Pour ½ cup of boiling water or hot apple cider into the cup, then stir until the spice mixture has dissolved completely.

3. Finish with a splash of half-and-half or heavy cream, if you'd like, and stir again. After tasting, add more water, cider, or cream, if needed.

4. Garnish with a sprinkling of ground cinnamon.

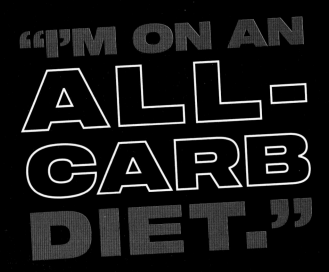

"I'M ON AN ALL-CARB DIET."

"It burns carbs.
It just burns up all your carbs."

Kälteen *Bar*

SERVES 1

2 tablespoons pureed banana
2 teaspoons peanut butter
  powder
5 ounces skim milk
banana slices, to garnish

1. Put all the ingredients into a cocktail shaker filled with ice cubes.

2. Shake hard and pour directly from the shaker into a highball glass.

3. Garnish with banana slices.

Winter Talent Show

SERVES 4

2 cups milk
⅔ cup strong black coffee
1 cinnamon stick
2 extra-large eggs
⅓ cup granulated sugar
½ cup heavy cream
2 teaspoons ground cinnamon

1. Put the milk, coffee, and cinnamon stick into a saucepan and heat over medium heat until almost boiling. Cool for 5 minutes, then remove and discard the cinnamon stick.

2. Put the eggs and sugar into a bowl and beat until pale and thick. Gradually beat in the milk and coffee mixture. Return to the pan and heat gently, stirring, until just thickened. Cool for 30 minutes.

3. Put the cream into a bowl and whip until it holds soft peaks. Gently fold the cream into the egg mixture. Divide among four glasses, sprinkle with ground cinnamon. Chill for 1–2 hours before serving.

CHAPTER SIX

Spring Fling

Throw your own Spring Fling with these recipes that feature botanical notes and aromatic flavors.

"I'm gonna vote for Regina George because she got hit by that bus."

"I'm voting for Cady Heron because she pushed her."

Spring Fling Queen

SERVES 10

48 ounces cranberry juice
15 ounces water
1½ teaspoons ground ginger
¾ teaspoon cinnamon
¾ teaspoon freshly grated
   nutmeg
frozen cranberries and their
   leaves, to garnish

1. Put the first five ingredients into a large saucepan or pot and bring to a boil. Reduce the heat and simmer for 5 minutes.

2. Remove from the heat and pour into a heatproof pitcher or bowl. Chill in the refrigerator.

3. Remove from the refrigerator, put ice into the serving glasses, pour in the punch, and garnish with cranberries and their leaves on cocktail sticks.

A Piece of the Crown

SERVES 2

2 teaspoons raspberry syrup
16 ounces chilled apple juice
fresh raspberries, to garnish
apple pieces, to garnish

1. Add ice and 1 teaspoon of raspberry syrup to each glass.

2. Fill each glass with 8 ounces of apple juice and stir well.

3. Garnish with the raspberries and pieces of apple.

"A piece for Gretchen Wieners, a partial Spring Fling Queen.

A piece for Janis Ian.

And a piece for Regina George. She fractured her spine, and she still looks like a rock star."

YOU GO, GLEN COCO

SERVES 1

2 teaspoons pineapple juice
2 tablespoons coconut water
3½ ounces ginger ale
2 kiwi slices, to garnish
pineapple leaf, to garnish

Kiwi Shrub
15 kiwis, peeled and quartered
1¾ cups sugar
12 ounces cider vinegar

This recipe includes a shrub that needs to be made ahead of time—plan accordingly.

1. To make the kiwi shrub, add the kiwi to a bowl with the sugar, and mix well. Cover and chill in the refrigerator for 1 hour.

2. Muddle the mixture, re-cover, and leave in the refrigerator overnight.

3. Strain the mixture and add the vinegar, then shake well and leave in the refrigerator overnight again. Strain through a cheese cloth or fine sieve and store in the refrigerator in a clean jar for up to one week.

4. Put 2 tablespoons of the kiwi shrub into a cocktail shaker with the pineapple juice, coconut water, and ice cubes, and shake well.

5. Strain into a highball glass filled with ice cubes. Top with the ginger ale and gently stir.

6. Garnish with kiwi slices and a pineapple leaf.

"AND NONE FOR GRETCHEN WIENERS."

"Two years ago she told me that hoop earrings were her thing and that I wasn't allowed to wear them anymore."

White-Gold Hoops

SERVES 2

11 ounces chilled fresh tea
4 ounces orange juice
4 tablespoons lime juice
1–2 tablespoons sugar
lime wedges
orange slices, to garnish

1. Add the orange juice, lime juice, and sugar, to taste, to the tea.

2. Take two glasses and rub the rims with a lime wedge, then dip them in sugar to frost.

3. Fill the glasses with ice and pour in the tea. Garnish with slices of orange.

Coolness

SERVES 2

6 ounces orange juice
6 ounces sparkling white grape
   juice
orange slices, to garnish

1. Chill two champagne flutes.

2. Divide the orange juice between the flutes and top with the sparkling grape juice.

3. Garnish with the orange slices.

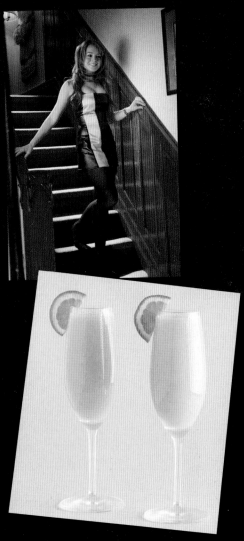

MORNING WEATHER ANNOUNCEMENTS

SERVES 1

1½ ounces orange juice
1½ ounces pineapple juice
1½ ounces lime juice
¾ ounce raspberry syrup
4 crushed fresh mint leaves
ginger ale
fresh mint sprig, to garnish

1. Shake the first five ingredients vigorously over ice until well frosted.

2. Strain into a chilled collins glass, top with ginger ale, and stir gently. Garnish with mint sprig.

Rainbows
and
Smiles

SERVES 1

2 ounces raspberry puree
6 ounces peach juice
sparkling water

1. In a cocktail shaker, shake the raspberry puree and peach juice over ice vigorously until well frosted.

2. Strain into a chilled tumbler, top with sparkling water, and stir gently.

"I JUST HAVE A LOT OF FEELINGS."

SHE DOESN'T EVEN GO HERE

SERVES 1

handful spinach leaves
¼ cup coconut flesh
7 ounces chilled water
½ cup cantaloupe, peeled,
   seeded, and chopped
1 tablespoon chopped
   fresh mint
juice of ½ lime
¼ cup mango, peeled, stoned,
   and chopped, plus 1 extra
   slice to garnish

1. Place the spinach, coconut, and water in a blender, and blend until smooth.

2. Add the melon, mint, lime juice, and mango, and blend until smooth and creamy.

3. Pour over crushed ice and serve, garnished with a mango slice.

Channeled Rage

SERVES 1

1½ ounces apple juice
1½ ounces pear juice
3 ounces cranberry juice
pink lemonade or cherry-
    flavored sparkling water
fresh or maraschino cherries,
    to garnish
pineapple wedge, to garnish

1. Mix the fruit juices together over ice in a chilled glass.

2. Fill with lemonade or sparkling water to taste and garnish with cherries and pineapple.

"Regina's spine healed, and her physical therapist taught her to channel all her rage into sports. It was perfect, because the jock girls weren't afraid of her."

The Limit
DOES NOT EXIST

SERVES 1

3 ounces passion fruit juice
3 ounces guava juice
3 ounces orange juice
1½ ounces coconut milk
1–2 teaspoon ginger syrup
slice of papaya, to garnish

1. Shake all the fruit juices
   with the coconut milk
   and ginger syrup with
   ice until well frosted.

2. Strain into a chilled
   highball glass or tall wine
   glass and garnish with
   a thin slice of papaya.

"If the limit never approaches anything... The limit does not exist.

The limit does not exist!"

Peace in Girl World

SERVES 1

1½ ounces pineapple juice
1½ ounces orange juice
¾ ounce lime juice
1½ ounces passion fruit
  juice
3 ounces guava juice
edible flower, to garnish

1. Shake together all the juices with crushed ice.

2. Strain into a chilled tall glass and garnish with an edible flower.

"Finally, Girl World was at peace.

And if any freshmen tried to disturb that peace, well, let's just say we knew how to take care of it."

INDEX

Published by Cottage Door Press, LLC
5005 Newport Drive
Rolling Meadows, Illinois 60008
www.cottagedoorpress.com

The cover shows *Axe Wound*, page 72; *The Plastics*, page 27; and *Karen*, page 37
Food photography by Mike Cooper and Günter Beer
Illustrations and additional food photography used under license from Shutterstock.com

ISBN 979-8-89019-019-2

The Art of Mixology™ logo is a trademark of Cottage Door Press, LLC.
www.artofmixology.com

Parragon Books is an imprint of Cottage Door Press, LLC.
Parragon® and the Parragon® logo are registered trademarks of Cottage Door Press, LLC.

All product names, logos, and brands are property of their respective owners. All company, product, and service names used in this book are for identification purposes only.
Use of these names, logos, and brands does not imply endorsement.

Note for the Reader

Unless otherwise stated, milk is assumed to be whole, eggs are large, and individual produce are medium-sized. People with allergies and intolerances (nut, dairy, grain, etc.) should be aware that some of the ingredients used in the recipes in this book may contain allergens and they should be prepared to substitute ingredients in accordance with their dietary requirements. Some specialty ingredients may need to be sourced from specialty stores but we encourage you to do your own research and try alternative ingredients or feel free to treat as an optional ingredient in said recipe. Recipes using raw or very lightly cooked eggs should be avoided by infants, the elderly, pregnant women, and people with weakened immune systems.

Garnishes, decorations, and serving suggestions are all optional and not necessarily included in the recipe ingredients or method. The times given are only an approximate guide. Preparation times differ according to the techniques used by different people and the cooking times may also vary from those given. Optional ingredients, variations, or serving suggestions have not been included in the time calculations.